One Hundred Days (Plus One)

For Becky
—M. M.

SIMON SPOTLIGHT
An imprint of Simon & Schuster Children's Publishing Division
1230 Avenue of the Americas New York, NY 10020
This Simon Spotlight edition August 2023
First Aladdin Paperbacks edition January 2003
Text copyright © 2003 by Simon & Schuster
Illustrations copyright © 2003 by Mike Gordon
All rights reserved, including the right of reproduction in whole or in part in any form.
SIMON SPOTLIGHT, READY-TO-READ, and colophon are
registered trademarks of Simon & Schuster, Inc
For information about special discounts for bulk purchases,
please contact Simon & Schuster Special Sales at 1-866-506-1949 or
business@simonandschuster.com.
Manufactured in the United States of America 0723 LAK
2 4 6 8 10 9 7 5 3 1
Cataloging-in-Publication Data was previously supplied for the paperback edition of this
title from the Library of Congress.
Library of Congress Cataloging-in-Publication Data:
McNamara, Margaret.
One hundred days (plus one) / by Margaret McNamara ; illustrated by Mike Gordon.—
p. cm. — (Robin Hill School)
Summary: Hannah looks forward to Robin Hill School's celebration of one hundred
days of classes, but when a cold keeps her home the day of the party she decides to
bring in the one hundred buttons she found anyway.
978-1-6659-3900-3 (hc)
978-0-689-85535-1 (pbk)
[1. Schools—Fiction. 2. Buttons—Fiction. 3. Counting.] I. Gordon, Mike, ill. II. Title.
PZ7.M232518 On 2003
[E]—dc21
2002008834

Robin Hill School

One Hundred Days (Plus One)

Written by Margaret McNamara
Illustrated by Mike Gordon

Ready-to-Read

Simon Spotlight
New York   London   Toronto   Sydney   New Delhi

Hannah was excited.

Only one week to go
until the party
to celebrate one hundred
days in school.

"That is a long time
to be in school,"
said Hannah.

Mrs. Connor told the class,
"Next Friday, please bring
in one hundred
little things
to share."

Hannah decided
to bring in buttons.

On Monday Hannah found
twenty white buttons.

On Tuesday she found
fifty-seven mixed buttons.

On Wednesday
she found
four cat buttons,
six diamond buttons,

and thirteen buttons
with no holes.

On Thursday Hannah counted her buttons from one to one hundred.

CHOOOOO

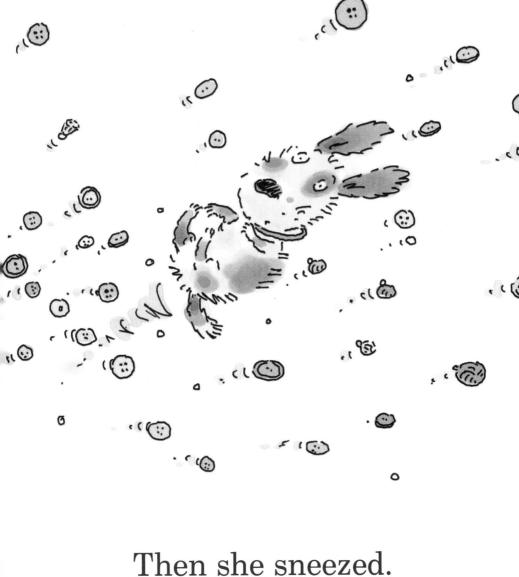

Then she sneezed.

On Friday
Hannah had a cold.
"No school for you today,"
said her mother.
"On Monday you will
feel better."

On Monday I will feel
worse, thought Hannah.

The party is today.
And I am not there.

On Monday Hannah's cold
was gone.

She wore her favorite
sweater to school.
It had one big orange button.

Hannah remembered
the one hundred buttons.

She put them
in her backpack,
even though she had
missed the party.

When the school bell rang,
Mrs. Connor said,
"Today is a special day.
What is one hundred
plus one?"

Hannah knew the answer.
"One hundred and one!"
she said.

"Right!" said Mrs. Connor.

"Today we have been in school
for one hundred and one days."
Hannah's friends were smiling.

They showed
101 grains of rice,

101 hair ribbons,

and 101 postcards.

"I only brought in
one hundred buttons,"
said Hannah.

"I did not think
to bring in one more,"
she said.

She remembered the button
on her sweater.
"Here is my plus one!"
she said.

"I thought one hundred days
was a long time
to go to school,"
said Hannah.

"And now I have gone
for one hundred plus one!"